DATE DUE

647.94
Qui
Quinlan, Kathryn A.

Food service manager

Careers without College

Food Service Manager

by *Kathryn A. Quinlan*

Julie Flik
President-elect
Society for Foodservice Management

CAPSTONE
HIGH/LOW BOOKS
an imprint of Capstone Press
Mankato, Minnesota

Capstone High/Low Books are published by Capstone Press
818 North Willow Street • Mankato, Minnesota 56001
http://www.capstone-press.com

Library of Congress Cataloging-in-Publication Data
Quinlan, Kathryn A.
    Food service manager/by Kathryn A. Quinlan.
        p. cm.—(Careers without college)
    Includes bibliographical references and index.
    Summary: Outlines the educational requirements, duties, salary, employment outlook,
and possible future positions for restaurant and food service managers.
    ISBN 0-7368-0034-4
    1. Food service management—Vocational guidance—Juvenile literature.
2. Restaurant management—Vocational guidance—Juvenile literature. [1. Food service
management—Vocational guidance. 2. Vocational guidance.] I. Title. II. Series.
TX911.3.V62Q55 1999
647.94'023—dc21   98-22672
                                                                                          CIP
                                                                                           AC

Editorial Credits
Kimberly J. Graber and Angela Kaelberer, editors; James Franklin, cover designer
    and illustrator; Sheri Gosewisch, photo researcher

Photo Credits
David F. Clobes, 9, 14, 16, 20, 22, 26, 32, 38, 44
David Stembridge, 11
International Stock Photo/Stan Pak, 18; Randy Masser, 36
Leslie O'Shaughnessy, 4, 6, 12, 28
Photri/Microstock/Jeff Greenberg, 30
Unicorn Stock Photos/Jeff Greenberg, cover, 35, 41; Jean Higgins, 24

Table of Contents

Fast Facts

Career Title_____ Food service manager

Minimum Educational _____ U.S.: high school diploma
Requirement   Canada: community college diploma

Certification Requirement _____ U.S.: none
                                  Canada: none

Salary Range_____ U.S.: $12,480 to $46,800
(U.S. Bureau of Labor Statistics and   Canada: $11,500 to $64,000
Human Resources Development Canada,
late 1990s figures)   (Canadian dollars)

Job Outlook _____ U.S.: faster than average growth
(U.S. Bureau of Labor Statistics and   Canada: fair
Human Resources Development
Canada, late 1990s projections)

DOT Cluster_____ Professional, technical, and
(Dictionary of Occupational Titles)   managerial occupations

DOT Number_____ 187.167-106

GOE Number_____ 11.11.04
(Guide for Occupational Exploration)

NOC_____ 0631
(National Occupational Classification—Canada)

Chapter 1

Job Responsibilities

Food service managers oversee restaurants and other places that serve food. Food service managers plan meals, order food and supplies, manage workers, and keep records. They make sure dining places follow laws for handling food and serving drinks. They make sure customers are satisfied with their food and service. Customers pay for goods, food, or service. Some food service

Food service managers oversee restaurants and other places that serve food.

managers are responsible for paying business expenses and workers' salaries.

Managers of large dining places usually are called general managers. General managers often have assistant managers to help with some management tasks. Executive chefs also may assist general managers. Executive chefs oversee kitchens and manage kitchen workers.

Managing Workers

Managers oversee people in many types of food service jobs. Chefs and cooks prepare food. Servers wait on tables and serve food. Host staff seat diners at tables. Bus staff clear tables, wash dishes, and clean dining establishments. Some places have bartenders who mix and serve drinks.

Food service managers hire, train, and manage all workers. Managers make sure workers arrive at work on time. They make sure workers are polite and offer customers good service.

Food service managers schedule the times when employees work.

Food service managers schedule the times when employees work. Managers must schedule the right number of workers for each shift. Customers receive poor service if managers schedule too few people to work. Dining places lose money if managers schedule too many workers.

Food service managers use estimates to decide how many people should work during each shift. Managers make this guess based on experience. They estimate how many customers will visit dining places during each shift. For example, a manager may know that Friday nights usually are busy. The manager may schedule extra staff to work the Friday night shift.

Planning Menus

Many food service managers plan menus. A menu is a list of food items a place serves. Some dining places use the same menu for long periods of time. Some add a few special meals or food items to their menus each night. Others regularly change their entire menus. Executive chefs in large dining places also may plan menus. They may work with managers to plan menus.

Managers try to offer food items customers will enjoy. They consider how popular items have been

Many food service managers plan menus.

in the past. They offer new food items so their customers will not become bored with the menu.

Food service managers in schools, hospitals, and nursing homes must plan nutritious meals. A nutritious meal contains elements the body uses

to stay strong and healthy. Fruits and vegetables are nutritious. Food service managers sometimes must plan menus for people who follow special diets. For example, some people cannot eat sugar. Others cannot eat spicy foods.

Ordering Food and Supplies

Food service managers order food. They study their menus before ordering food. Managers must order all the ingredients needed to make the food items on their menus.

Managers try to order exactly the right amount of food. Some food is wasted if managers order too much. Dining places are unable to serve all their customers if managers do not order enough food. Managers estimate how much food will be served each day. They also check their inventories to see how much of each ingredient they already have. An inventory is a list of all the items in stock.

Many restaurants have point-of-service (POS) systems. A POS system is a computer system that helps a restaurant keep records. Servers enter

Food service managers check their inventories to see how much of each ingredient they already have.

Food service managers check the portion sizes and quality of prepared meals.

customers' orders into a POS system. The system's computer sends the orders to the kitchen. The computer creates and prints the customers' bills. It subtracts the food items from the restaurant's inventory at the same time. Managers can check their POS systems to see how much food is left after each day or shift.

Food service managers also order supplies. Supplies include tablecloths, glasses, and silverware. Managers check their supply inventories regularly to see what they should order.

Assuring Quality

Food service managers check the portion sizes and quality of prepared meals. They make sure portion sizes are about the same for every meal. They make sure the food looks and tastes good. Managers also make sure workers serve the food on time and at the proper temperature.

Food service managers make sure that workers handle food properly. Food that is not handled safely can make people sick. The U.S. government works with state and local governments to set standards for handling food. Managers make sure food service workers follow these standards.

Managers have several ways to check that food is safe. Meats are safe if they are cooked to certain temperatures. Workers wash fruits and vegetables

well to remove dirt and illness-causing bacteria. Managers also instruct workers to clean dishes and silverware properly. They make sure workers wash their hands before handling food.

Administrative Duties

Food service managers perform the administrative duties needed to keep a business running. These duties include keeping track of the hours people work. Managers also may hire people to repair and maintain machines, remove waste, and control pests.

Managers keep track of the money dining places earn from customers. Dining places should earn more money than they spend. Managers pay workers. They pay people who bring food and supplies. They also pay business taxes. Managers must find ways to cut costs if bills are too high.

Managers often are responsible for closing dining places at the end of a day. They lock the doors and check that ovens and lights are off. They turn on alarm systems. They deposit money in the bank or put it in a secure place.

Managers often are responsible for closing dining places at the end of a day.

Chapter 2

What the Job Is Like

Food service managers work in many different settings. Some oversee restaurants. Others manage cafeterias where people serve themselves or are served at a counter. Schools, factories, office buildings, and department stores often have cafeterias. Some food service managers work in nursing homes or hospitals.

Some food service managers work for food service companies. These companies manage food services for many hospitals, schools, airlines, and

Some food service managers work in nursing homes or hospitals.

Food service managers spend a great deal of time talking with people.

large companies. Food service companies help these places provide food for patients, students, passengers, or workers.

Work Environment

Food service managers work many hours. They usually arrive at work before other staff members. They often leave work after other staff members. Managers may fill in for people who cannot come to work.

Many food service managers work more than 50 hours per week. They often work nights and weekends. Food service managers in factories and offices may work during the day.

Food service managers often experience pressure in their jobs. Managers must oversee many activities at one time. They must solve problems without affecting service to customers. Managers may serve, cook, or clear tables when dining places are busy.

Food service managers face some risks at work. Managers may handle hot dishes and pans or work near people who do. They sometimes work near hot grills. Floors can become slippery when people spill food or liquids.

Working with Staff and Customers

Food service managers spend a great deal of time talking with people. They try to keep both workers and customers happy.

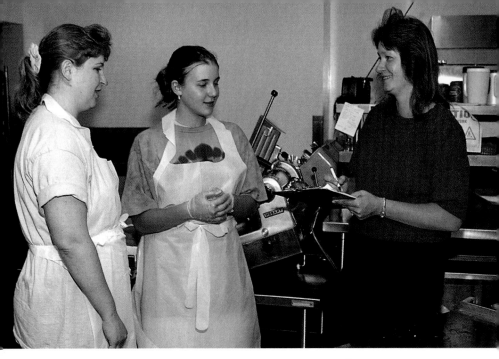

Food service managers keep food service teams working smoothly.

Food service staff members work in teams. One cook might grill a steak for a meal while another cook fixes the vegetables. The cooks tell the servers when food is ready to be served. Servers move quickly to serve food while it is hot.

Managers keep these teams working smoothly. They help workers solve differences with each other. They make sure everyone's work load is equal.

Food service managers also talk to customers. Managers try to fix problems if customers are unhappy. For example, customers might be unhappy because their food is cold. A manager might ask the cooks to fix new meals for those customers. Managers try to make sure customers enjoy their meals enough to come back.

Personal Qualities

Food service managers must have both people skills and business skills. They should be good leaders. Managers should be able to make customers feel important. They should be good at keeping records and managing money. They also should be able to solve problems.

Food service managers must be able to make hard decisions. They must be able to hire and fire workers.

Managers should be healthy. They work many hours and do some carrying and lifting. They must have the energy and strength to do something for a long time.

Chapter 3

Training

Many people prepare to become food service managers by working in restaurants or other food service settings. They usually start working as servers or cooks. Workers can advance to be assistant managers as they gain experience.

Managers who work for chain restaurants and food service companies often train on the job. Chain restaurants have the same name and serve the same food in many locations. Training may last six months to one year on the job. Workers advance to assistant manager after they complete

Many people become food service managers by working in restaurants.

their training. Assistant managers can later advance to managers.

Educational Programs

People with more education can start in higher management positions than those with less education. Some students enter food service management programs offered by community colleges and vocational colleges. These programs last about two to four years. The programs offer classes in accounting, business law, and management. They also offer classes in food planning, cooking, and nutrition.

Some food service management programs require students to work as interns. Students learn management skills from skilled food service managers during internships. This experience shows students how food service businesses work.

Some food service managers have bachelor's degrees. A bachelor's degree is a title given to a person for completing a course of study. People

Interns learn management skills from skilled food service managers.

usually can earn bachelor's degrees in four years. Food service managers may have degrees in food service management. They also may have degrees in other areas. For example, some food service managers have degrees in business management.

Food service managers in Canada usually have community college diplomas. They study food service management or hospitality. Hospitality means receiving and entertaining guests. Food service managers in Canada also have several years of experience. Their experience usually includes overseeing other workers.

What Students Can Do Now

Students can gain experience by working in restaurants and cafeterias. They can work as servers or cashiers. They can help prepare food, wash dishes, or set and clear tables.

Each of these jobs helps students learn about food service work. Students learn to work in teams and work with customers. They also find out if they enjoy the fast pace of food service work.

Students can gain experience by working in restaurants and cafeterias.

Chapter 4

Salary and Job Outlook

The average full-time food service manager in the United States earns $16,640 to $32,760 per year (all figures late 1990s). Managers who work in small restaurants or have little experience may earn just over $12,000. Managers who work in large restaurants or have more experience may earn up to $46,800.

Full-time food service managers in Canada earn an average of about $37,000 per year. Beginning

Managers who work in large restaurants or have more experience usually earn higher salaries.

31

managers earn about $11,500. Experienced
managers may earn up to $64,000.

Food service managers' salaries can vary
depending on their jobs. Managers of expensive
restaurants earn higher salaries than managers of
less expensive restaurants. Managers of large
dining places earn higher salaries than managers
of small dining places. Managers who work in
large cities usually earn more than managers who
work in small towns. Food service managers also
earn more money in large hospitals, schools, and
nursing homes.

Benefits

Food service managers usually receive benefits.
Dining places may provide free meals, health
insurance, paid vacation, and sick leave as
benefits. Health insurance is protection from the
costs of getting sick or injured. Dining places pay
money to insurance companies each month. The

**Food service managers' salaries can vary depending
on their jobs.**

insurance companies pay most of the medical bills if workers become sick or injured.

Many managers also earn extra money in bonuses each year. Food service managers' bonuses may range from $2,000 to $10,000.

Job Outlook

Food service management is a growing field in the United States. People who work hard and have experience can expect to find many job openings. Opportunities are best for those with education.

The food service management field is growing in the United States for several reasons. Many families have little time to cook at home. They also may earn slightly higher incomes than in the past if both parents work. This means more people eat at restaurants today than in the past. Food service managers also find job opportunities in nursing homes and senior centers. This is because the number of older people is increasing in the United States.

Food service managers are finding opportunities in nursing homes and senior centers.

The job outlook for food service managers in Canada is fair. Most new food service jobs probably will result from workers who change careers or retire. Managers with computer skills will find the most job opportunities. This is because the use of computers in food service management is expected to increase.

Chapter 5

Where the Job Can Lead

Most food service managers advance as they gain experience. They may earn raises and bonuses if the dining places they manage do well. Managers also may advance by taking jobs with larger dining places. Some food service managers advance to oversee several schools, hospitals, or restaurants.

Managers may have more opportunities if they are willing to move. Large cities usually have

Food service managers may advance by taking jobs with larger dining places.

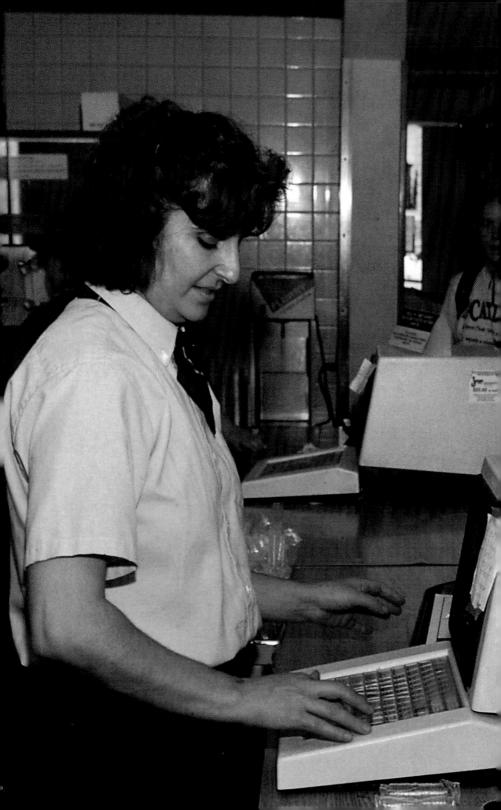

more job openings than small towns. Cities usually have jobs with more responsibility than jobs in small towns.

Food Service Management Professionals

A manager in the United States may choose to become a Foodservice Management Professional (FMP). The Educational Foundation of the National Restaurant Association awards this title. Food service managers do not need the FMP title to work or to advance. But employers recognize people who have this title as good managers.

Managers must meet several requirements to receive the FMP title. They must reach certain work standards before they can even apply for the title. Managers with no formal food service education must have more work experience than managers with degrees. Managers also must take courses in food service. Applicants who meet education and work requirements then must pass a test to receive the FMP title.

Chain restaurant managers may advance to oversee all the restaurants in an area as regional managers.

Other Opportunities

Some food service managers change jobs to advance. For example, they may advance to manage the food service operations of hotels, resorts, or cruise ships.

Some food service managers decide to buy restaurants. It is risky to own a restaurant. Owners lose their money if their restaurants fail. But owners can earn a great deal of money if their restaurants do well. Managers often succeed as owners because they know how to run restaurants smoothly.

Food service managers may advance to manage food service operations of hotels, resorts, or cruise ships.

Words to Know

bacteria (bak-TIHR-ee-uh)—one-celled, microscopic living things that may cause illnesses

benefit (BEN-uh-fit)—a payment or service in addition to a salary or a wage

bonus (BOH-nuhss)—extra money a worker receives for doing a good job

cafeteria (kaf-uh-TIHR-ee-uh)—a restaurant in which people serve themselves or are served at a counter

customer (KUHSS-tuh-mur)—a person who pays for goods, food, or services

estimate (ESS-ti-muht)—a guess based on experience

hospitality (hoss-puh-TAL-uh-tee)—to receive and entertain guests

intern (IN-turn)—a person who learns a skill or job by working with someone in that field

inventory (IN-vuhn-tor-ee)—a list of all the items in stock

menu (MEN-yoo)—a list of food items and drinks a dining place serves

nutritious (noo-TRISH-uhss)—containing elements the body uses to stay strong and healthy

schedule (SKEJ-ul)—to plan when people work

To Learn More

Beal, Eileen. *Choosing a Career in the Restaurant Industry.* World of Work. New York: Rosen Publishing Group, 1997.

Chmelynski, Carol Ann Caprione. *Opportunities in Restaurant Careers.* VGM Opportunities. Lincolnwood, Ill.: VGM Career Horizons, 1998.

Cosgrove, Holli, ed. *Career Discovery Encyclopedia,* vol. 3. Chicago: J. G. Ferguson Publishing, 1997.

Streissguth, Tom. *Getting Ready for a Career in Food Service.* Getting Ready for Careers. Minneapolis, Minn.: Capstone Press, 1996.

Useful Addresses

**Canadian Restaurant and
    Foodservices Association**
316 Bloor Street West
Toronto, Ontario M5S 1W5
Canada

**Educational Foundation of the National
    Restaurant Association**
250 South Wacker Drive
Suite 1400
Chicago, IL 60606-5834

Society for Foodservice Management
304 West Liberty Street
Suite 201
Louisville, KY 40202

Internet Sites

Canada Job Futures
http://www.hrdc-drhc.gc.ca/JobFutures/english/
  volume1/063/063.htm

**Food Safety at Home, School and When
Eating Out**
http://www.foodsafety.gov/~dms/cbook.html

National Restaurant Association
http://www.restaurant.org/

**Occupational Outlook Handbook—
Restaurant and Food Service Managers**
http://stats.bls.gov/oco/ocos024.htm

Society for Foodservice Management Cafe
http://www.sfm-online.org/

Index